Tigress

By
TL KATT

A story from the Winter
Thrillz Collection.

This book is a work of fiction. Any characters or events are purely figments of the author's imagination.

Tigress

Copyright © 2019 TL Katt
ISBN: 978-1-951017-05-7
Cover Design: TL Katt
Editor: Dawn Lewis

Published by Books by Elle, Inc.
225 College Dr. #65504
Orange Park, FL 32065
www.elleklass.weebly.com

Chapter 1

Jestin turned his truck onto the gravel road, the snow around him dusting the earth beneath the tires. The snowy retreat just what he needed after defending the asshole he knew had killed his wife in cold blood. It was his job. Times like these, he wished he stood on the other side, defending the victim, but many times the defendant was the victim. DNA now proved so many people were wrongly convicted, and then there were the ones like Trevor Bolling.

The evidence was all circumstantial, nothing tied him to the murder and he conjured real tears when his wife's name came up. He did his job and Trevor's case was dropped. It was his demeanor, the smirk on his face, the twisting of his hands, and his arrogant attitude. If he'd put him on the stand, his attitude alone would have convicted him. But his job was to defend his client, guilty or innocent.

The snow falling faster now, making Jestin creep his vehicle over the snowy gravel toward the cabin at a snail's pace. A light dusting now covered the trees. His phone beeped, causing him to look away from the road for a second. His eyes scanned the message, work related. He dropped the phone onto the passenger seat, not willing to work when he was on vacation. The purpose of the trip was to get away from work and stress.

When he lifted his eyes to the road, a white flash in front of him

Tigress

caught his attention. "What the..." His voice trailed off as he stopped the car and got out, thinking maybe he'd hit something. A fresh set of paw prints crossed the road from one side of the woods to the other. Not much of a hunter, he wasn't sure what type of animal. From his trips to the zoo as a child, they looked to him like tiger prints -- but tigers didn't exist in Virginia except in the zoo. Scratching his head, he got back into the car and continued up the snow-laden road.

He thought of all the animals that lived in these woods; black bears, foxes, raccoons, deer, and skunks. It wasn't any of those. A wolf maybe. *Did they inhabit the woods here?*

A majestic white animal stared at him as he studied the ground then resumed his drive. Its violet eyes narrowed.

Chapter 2

*J*estin pulled into the horseshoe drive of the cabin and stepped out of the vehicle, sucking in the clean, chilly air surrounding him. His eyes scanning the area for animals, namely the one he was sure he'd seen but nothing except quiet and snow-covered trees.

He stretched and opened the back door of his oversized truck, reached in and pulled out his luggage, carrying it up

the small covered porch
to the front door. He
dropped it and fiddled
with his key in the lock. A
crackling sound from the
woods forced him to
twist his head in that
direction. He saw
nothing. The sound was
barely audible, it was
nothing.

Inside, he dropped
his bag. Leaving the door
open, he made a couple
trips to and from his car,
his arms filled with
groceries. The air outside
growing dark, he went to
the shed before the sun
set completely for the day
and grabbed an armful of

firewood. The cabin inside was cold and he needed to get the fire roaring before the temperature dropped further. The snow now inches thick, he trudged to the cabin and laid the load of wood near the fireplace, then considered if he should get more. The snow outside now coming down much heavier than earlier.

Even inside his thick coat, he shivered and decided against bringing in more wood now; he'd do it in the morning. Locking the door and dropping the bar across it, he went straight to building a fire. Warmth first, food second.

Three hours later, he finished dinner, took a bite off a piece of cornbread that went with the chili he'd made and stared blankly into the snow. The white flash of the animal he'd seen earlier high on his thought list. There wasn't one white animal he could think of that lived in the woods, unless it was a wolf. It had to be a wolf, which meant there were more. Wolves weren't singular animals but plural, they moved in packs.

A shotgun leaned against the log wall beside the door. He had protection if it was a wolf. He didn't hunt but could fire a bullet straight into the heart or head of anything. His dad had taught him since he was a boy, hoping to make him a hunter. Jestin didn't have the heart. He was a softie who loved life. Again, the case with Trevor Bolling haunted him.

Drawing open the curtain in his room so the sun would shine bright in the morning and wake him early, he lay in bed, fighting his thoughts about work, and went to sleep.

His sleep burdened with his own guilt, he tossed and turned, finally waking. The light of the crescent moon filtering through the window, casting a glow. Fluffing the pillow beneath his head, he turned toward the open window, two violet eyes stared back at him.

Chapter 3

His breath caught in his throat and his heart skipped a few beats. As he jumped to his feet in one swift movement, the eyes disappeared. Was it his imagination?

His breathing returned to normal as he sat on the edge of the bed. The snow outside now much thicker but no longer falling. He stood and padded towards the window, there was

nothing outside. Jestin
drew the curtain closed,
then changed his mind.
*What the hell was he scared
of?* Empty, snow-covered
woods surrounded him
and he was safe inside his
cabin. A chill traveled up
his spine as he realized he
stood in only cotton
briefs and the air was a bit
nippy.

In the living room,
he stoked the fire and
took a seat in the worn
recliner. He pulled a
thermal blanket over his
legs. Too many thoughts
coasted through his brain
for sleep, so he picked up
a novel and read.

Tigress

Eventually, his eyes grew weary and sleep took him.

The bright sunlight woke him a few hours later as it shone across the cabin. He stretched and traipsed to his bedroom to get dressed. In the kitchen, he started a pot of coffee, then pulled on his snow boots to get more wood.

When he opened the door, the light from the sun glinting off the pure white, powdery snow blinded him, so he grabbed his sunglasses and went onto the porch, then down the couple steps and towards the shed. Grabbing the wood, he carried it back to the cabin, then went back for more. His second trip, he gazed to his left at the bedroom window and noticed an indent in the snowy ground below it. Dropping the wood onto the porch, he cautiously moved toward the window. A trail of paw prints went from the window into the woods. He followed them until he reached the tree line, where they disappeared.

Twisting his lips. He trudged back to the cabin, grabbed a cup of coffee, and whipped up eggs and pancakes. Gulping them down, he bundled into his coat and boots, then grabbed his shotgun. Once more, he followed the paw prints into the woods on the lookout for the animal. If it was a wolf, he didn't want to meet it face to face without protection. *What are you doing?* he questioned himself. *You're not a hunter, get back to the safety of the cabin and forget this nonsense. You're safe from predators inside.* He turned on his heel and trudged back to the cabin.

Unable to concentrate on his novel

and relaxing, he picked up his phone to call the game warden, but when he saw his signal had disappeared -- as should be expected in the mountainous terrain that lacked an abundance of cell towers -- he set the phone down. This was his retreat; no signal, no service, no internet, no TV. He was escaping life.

A few of his father's books lay on a wooden wall shelf. He glanced at their titles; *Wildlife in Virginia* and *Hunting for the Professional.* The first one caught his eye. All the times his father dragged him to the cabin attempting to make a hunter out of him, he'd never read the books or paid attention to the hunting lessons his father bestowed on him. Finally, at age fourteen, his father quit bringing him, realizing he had no desire to hunt even though he was an excellent marksman.

It was many a time he purposely messed up a shot to avoid hitting a deer or other animal, insisting to his father it was nerves. This was his first trip alone to the cabin since age fourteen and since his father's death.

Wolves weren't listed as an animal that roamed the woods, nor were coyotes or any four-legged beast large enough to have made the prints. Engrossed in the book, he didn't hear the creaking on the porch steps outside.

Chapter 4

loud knock at the door startled him out of his thoughts. Leaping off the chair, he rested a hand on his heart. *Who is here?* he questioned. Wild animals didn't knock, so it had to be human. Chuckling at himself, he padded toward the door and opened it.

A man he guessed to be around sixty, of medium height and build, with a beer belly and large straggly beard, stared at him. "I saw the smoke, thought Dan might be here," the man said, peering around Jestin as if looking for his father.

One of the mountain folk his father made friends with he assumed. "Dan is... was my father. He passed away several months ago from a blood infection."

The man's small eyes widened inside his roundish face. "Blood infection ya say?"

Jestin nodded. "A very rare illness and the medical journals had little info. Even the specialists were baffled."

"I'm sorry ta hear," voiced the man, taking a step backwards. "I'll leave ya to ya peace."

Jestin suddenly realized he didn't want to be alone and this man may have a few answers, or at least memories of his father. Something to occupy his time.

"Why don't you come in. I have homemade chili, cornbread. We can eat and chat. It'd be nice to have company. My name is Jestin."

"Hank," said the man, extending a bushy fat hand. "A friend of your father's. I reckon I'll take ya up on ya offer." The man's accent was strong and difficult to understand.

The men talked for a couple hours until the sun began to set, then Hank stood. "Thank ya, but I best be goin'. Not safe out thar at night and the old lady is waitin'."

That struck Jestin odd, remembering the paw prints and vision of violet eyes peering at him from outside the window. "Do wolves or coyotes inhabit these woods?"

The man chuckled. "No dogs, but there's

large cats that roam the Blue Ridge. Always thought my kin was crazy till a large cougar stared me down lickin' it's chops. I was a boy and my pappy shot the gun, whizzed over the top of tha animal and it skedaddled. No, I don't take no chances."

"Thanks for entertaining me Hank," Jestin said with a smile.

He bundled into his coat and boots. "My pleasure son." He paused for a second. "You a hunter like ya father?"

"No sir, I'm here to enjoy a quiet retreat. Takes the edge off."

Stepping onto the porch, Hank said, "Night."

Jestin watched the man leave. The book didn't say anything about cougars or pumas. Maybe it was just mountain legends.

Settling onto his recliner for the evening, he popped a beer and continued his novel, falling asleep in the chair. Scratching from the side of the cabin woke him with a start at one a.m.,

Tigress

his eyes shifting towards
the window.

Chapter 5

othing stared at him. Stretching, he lifted himself out of the chair, stoked the fire and moseyed to bed. It was only his imagination. Taking one last glance out the window, he noted the wind blowing a tree branch toward the cabin. Sighing deep, he lay on the bed, pulling the thick blanket to his chin.

The next day, he went into the shed and found a hatchet. He

shimmied up the tree and positioned himself on a large, hefty branch. From there, he chopped off the smaller branch that scratched at the cabin.

He positioned his recliner in front of the window, went about his business during the day, and fell asleep watching the woods at night. Nothing happened.

The following day, he again went about his business and fell asleep in his recliner, watching the outside. Nothing.

The third night after dinner, beef stew and rice, he went to bed. It was all in his mind, and Hank telling him cats roamed the woods. He'd worked himself up over nothing, however, he kept the curtains open. The sunlight was his time clock and if, by chance, any large animals did exist in the woods he was going to face them head on. After all, he did see the large paw prints. They weren't his imagination.

His sleep was restless and several hours later he awoke. Two violet eyes glared at him from the window. He blinked several times then rubbed his eyes, positive he was seeing things, but the eyes didn't vanish this time.

In a trance-like state, he arose from bed and walked toward the window. The violet eyes belonged to a magnificent animal. Its white fur visible in the first quarter moon. Its hot breath leaving fog on his window. He stood staring, unable to believe his eyes.

As if under a spell, he dressed and ran to the front door. Flinging it open, he looked towards the spot the animal had only moments ago occupied. Scanning the area, he saw a flurry of something undefinable and movement near the tree line.

He scrambled off his porch and through the woods, nearly tripping in the snow. Once he reached the tree line, he slowed and moved through the woods. Steam rising from the earth caught his attention and a woman, almost white as the snow and buck naked, stood before him. She was tiny, with breasts no larger than biscuits, and an oval face. Her blonde hair hung in curls around her shoulders and her eyes were a deep violet. The steam wasn't rising from the snow, but from her.

He took a step towards the woman. "Are you real?" he asked, more to himself.

She answered, "I am. Come." Her voice pulled him further towards her. He felt caught in the middle of reality and a dream.

"Pinch me," he demanded.

She moved toward him, her heat making him sweat inside his coat and he felt his cock rise inside his pants. Gently, she touched his arm and pinched a small piece of his cheek between her fingers.

The warmth of her hands tingled against his flesh, sending waves of desire through his body and a feeling of his face on fire when she let go.

"Ouch," he said.

She giggled. "You aren't dreaming."

A gun shot rang through the air and Jestin turned to see Hank standing a few feet away. "What are you doing out here?" he asked.

Jestin turned back towards the woman and

she was gone. Vanished.
"I was... I thought I saw
something here in the
woods."

"You didn't see
nothin' and if'n you did,
then you put your life in
danger."

If it was so
dangerous, what was
Hank doing in the woods
at night. "Why are you
out here?"

"My house is yonder.
I saw something moving
out here and find it's you.
Get yer ass home. I ain't
saving it more than once.
I did it this time for yer
father."

Jestin didn't argue with a man who held a shotgun. He trudged home to the cabin. The vision of the woman on his mind. She was beautiful with steam radiating off her tiny body. He wanted her, hoped she'd show herself again.

He fell asleep, her a vision in his mind. She dominated his dreams and her voice called to him, 'Come.'

Chapter 6

He woke with his hand wrapped around his hard cock, stroking. Her body etched in his mind. *Down boy*, he thought as he climbed out of bed and slipped on sweats.

He made his coffee, pulled a kitchen chair to the front porch and sat with his coffee mug. His eyes scanning the tree line. Maybe she'd been a dream. No, he convinced himself she was real and looked to the sky for smoke rising above the trees. Hank acted local enough, maybe he knew more than he let on. Sure enough, a small plume rose above and spread into the air. He set his empty mug down, locked the door, and walked into the woods.

As he drew further into the forest, he smelled the burning wood from a fireplace and continued. He hadn't smelled or noticed the night before, but then again, all he saw after meeting the naked woman in the woods was her.

Tigress

The scent told him he was close and a small log cabin appeared in the woods, buried amongst the trees. An old truck, circa 1950, stood outside the log house and a large shed stood behind the house. He proceeded towards the front door with caution. *What if it's not his house?*

He halted in front of the door and took a deep breath to prepare himself for whatever happened when he knocked on the door.

"Jestin," came a male voice behind him. He

turned to see Hank standing a few feet away.

Relieved, Jestin said, "Good morning. Can we talk?"

Hank sucked in a deep breath and nodded his head. "Take a seat." He pointed to a couple stumps arranged on his porch.

Jestin sat as Hank lumbered up the steps. "Last night, I saw something outside my window," he ran his hand through his thick dark hair, "I followed it into the woods."

Hank took a seat on the tree stump beside

him. "There are large cats
in these woods. I told you
that."

"This was a woman
with violet eyes."

Hank's eyes widened
and he wrung his hands
together. Jestin studied
his body language. There
was more to the story.

"Please, Hank. I need
to know."

He nodded, wrinkles
webbed across his face as
he spoke. "My kin's lived
in these woods for
generations. Thar is the
legend of a white tiger
who prowls the woods.
The stories have been
passed on and I never

believed 'em until I'd been near mauled by that cougar, but never seen a tiger. Your father, he'd seen it and wanted it as a trophy. I helped him search, telling him how absurd the stories were. He didn't listen. After tracking a cat for several days, we were deep in the woods. Night fell, but the full moon lighted the woods around us. A large white animal appeared out of the snow and leaped over yer father, knocking him down, its claws shredding the thick coat across his chest." He paused.

Tigress

Jestin clung to his words. "What happened next?"

Hank swallowed and continued. "I helped him up, bandaged him, and when we made it back home, he packed and left. I haven't seen him since. But I don't think he died of a rare blood disease. The white tiger killed him." His eyes shot down to the wooden boards beneath his feet. "The legends say the white cat only harms those who seek to harm her and her kin. Your father hunted her with the wrong intentions. I helped him.

The cat will find me too and I will die like yer father."

Jestin found the story far-fetched, then her violet eyes burned inside his head but it didn't make sense. "You live here. If this legend is true, why hasn't she killed you yet?"

He half-smiled. "She's nocturnal and I don't leave my home at night. My kin's stories say they lived at peace with her and she protected them, but harm her and the treaty is null and void."

Tigress

Jestin nodded, soaking in the man's words. "Does she have a name?"

"She is known to us only as Tigress."

The cold soaking into Jestin's bones. He'd heard enough and was ready to head home and heat himself by the fire. "Thank-you," he said as he stood.

"One more thang. The stories are old, but the legend is real. She is alive and roams the Blue Ridge," his brown eyes narrowed and his voice eerie.

Jestin hurried home,
the sun beginning to set.
He'd nap, then find
Tigress.

Chapter 7

"**C**ome," said her voice inside his head.

He ate his last bite of stew, then bundled in his coat and boots, all the while staring out the window. In the dark of night, he traveled into the woods. "Tigress," he called. "I won't hurt you. Show yourself to me again."

Something yellow glowed through the brush in the woods. Jestin focused on the glow which soon became two glowing yellow objects. Twigs crunched beneath the weight of something. He turned and two green objects glowed at him. More crunching and four blue objects shone through the woods, moving closer.

Jestin stood still, the glowing objects grew closer to him until he noted they were eyes. Inside, he felt peace around the creatures he knew instinctively he should fear. The glowing objects rose to eye level and four people walked out of the woods, surrounding him on all sides. Each naked, steam emanating from them.

The yellow-eyed one the largest. His body so defined, Jestin didn't see an ounce of fat anywhere on it. Yellow eyes moved forward, extending his hand. "You call the Tigress. Come."

Jestin followed without saying a word. Green eyes and the two blue-eyed men followed behind him. They all had muscles chiseled from stone, making Jestin glad he was fully clothed. His physique looked nothing like theirs. As a lawyer he worked 24/7 and skipped workouts most days. Even as a young active man he looked nothing like these men.

The moon provided enough light, especially as his eyes adjusted, to see a cave was just ahead.

Yellow eyes stopped. "Wait here," he demanded, his voice deep.

Jestin nodded and all the naked men entered the cave. An eerie feeling fell upon him as he realized he was alone in the woods. His back turned to the cave entrance, he stared at the moon, something soft as satin brushed against his hand. His fingers curled and he shifted his eyes downward. A large white tiger with violet eyes sat on its haunches in front of him. Their gaze met and, in front of his eyes, it changed, becoming the woman he'd seen.

"Tigress?" he asked in a whisper.

"I am known by that. My name is Kyanne." She brought her steaming hand to his face. "I have sought you since the prophecy of my elders," she said, whispering in his ear. Her face against his.

He felt his cock grow again and wanted her then and there. He'd never wanted anything as much as he did her at that moment. She lowered herself flat on her bare feet, her head level with his shoulder, the heat from her body making him sweat underneath all his clothing. She wiped a bead of sweat from his brow and brought it to her mouth, then licked.

"Come," she said in a breathy voice.

At this point he'd do anything she asked.

She grabbed his hand and guided him into the

cave. None of the men were there -- where had they gone? He pondered for a second but didn't care. His urge for her growing, he undid his coat and tossed it onto a rock in the cave as he followed her cute, heart-shaped ass further into the cave. In the darkness, only her eyes glowed as she turned towards him.

She lifted his hand. "This will hurt only for a moment, then you will feel euphoric," she stated.

He already felt euphoric and moved closer to her, grabbing her chin in his hand.

Lowering his head, he found her lips and kissed them. He moved his hand to her biscuit-sized breasts and rubbed against her nipples, along her stomach, then found her clit. Brushing his finger against it, precum oozed inside his pants.

She stepped backwards. "Not yet," she ordered.

"I want you now so much," he said. His voice raspy and his body shaking with need for her. Then a sharp pain caught the palm of his hand.

"Our blood has to mingle first."

Tigress

Bubbling blood covered his palm and he squeezed it shut. His eyebrows pinched into a question.

"Open it. You will not scar."

He released his palm and his hand was normal. The blood gone.

"My ancestors prophesied centuries ago that you would be my mate. A gentle, dark-haired man drawn to me during the crescent moon. His father a hunter, one who sought to destroy us."

He didn't care about the prophecy or the

legends and rambling stories of kinfolk. He only wanted her.

"Now?" he asked, drawing her toward him and folding her into his body so she could feel his full erection.

She didn't answer in words as her mouth found his and they kissed, their hands exploring each other. "You're so wet. I can't wait. I want you now," he whispered.

She bent on all fours, her ass displayed to him as he grabbed it and thrust his cock deep inside her vagina. He didn't feel the dirt floor beneath his knees. Euphoria wasn't the word for what he felt. After only a few thrusts, he came the first time, his seed spilling into her. He didn't care, as her screams of pleasure matched his moans, exciting him more.

They coupled several times, in many positions, until they exhausted each other and fell asleep entwined together.

Chapter 8

ometime later, he awoke, the spot beside him against the cave floor empty. He remembered clearly their night of sex but didn't remember the earth beneath them. He grabbed for his knees, expecting "rug burn", but they were smooth.

The sound of distant voices caught his attention and he rose to his feet and followed the voices through the dark cave to the opening. He saw several fuzzy forms, but the light was too intense. Shielding his eyes and squinting, he gazed towards them.

"You're awake," said a female voice. Then one of the fuzzy forms stood, walked towards him, and grabbed his package, stroking gentle and steady. He recognized the touch that sent a heatwave bolting through him. "Kyanne," he moaned. She licked his chest.

Oh no! He wanted her bad, but not in front of everyone. He tried to fight his ejaculation as her hand, soft to the touch, stroked and her warm, wet tongue slid over his body.

"Not now, please not now," he moaned. She wasn't stopping and he couldn't control his urges for her. He wrapped his arms around her waist and stepped her backwards into the darkness of the tunnels. Then he lifted her up, setting her against the wall and pounded into her; hard and furious.

Once they released again, his senses came back online. They'd had an unlimited amount of sex without protection. What was he thinking? Her head rested against his shoulder and he remembered he hadn't been thinking -- at least not with his brain.

"I'm sorry. I didn't use protection. I hope you're not--"

She raised her head and placed a finger over his mouth. "Shhh... if it is meant to be, then it will."

He felt himself growing again inside her. Not again. He needed answers, then he'd give the sexual beast inside him all it wanted with this beautiful and willing woman.

He stepped backwards and dropped her gently to her feet. Vaguely, he remembered her talking about a prophecy. He needed to know what he'd walked into. "Tell me about this prophecy."

Grabbing his hand, she led him back to the light. "This is all that's left of my family. We inhabited the mountains many centuries ago before humans took it over." His eyes adjusted as she spoke and distinguished four couples. A woman with

large breasts and sat
between green eyes' legs,
his arms wrapped around
her round, pregnant belly.
The blue-eyed pair, a man
and woman, were cuddled
in each other's arms, her
buttocks resting on his
legs. A dark-skinned
woman had her legs
wrapped around yellow
eyes, her ass against a
rock. The other blue-eyed
man was missing. He
didn't want to interrupt,
so made a mental note.

Kyanne's voice was
music to his ears as she
relayed the story. "We
made a partnership with
the first humans and lived

peacefully for many years but, over time, the younger generations no longer believed the stories. As you see, everyone has a partner and is able to reproduce. Zoe and Byzee have small cubs and rarely leave their presence. Once they are old enough you will see them." She spoke as if he was staying. He had a life to get back to… *or did he?* Would staying with her and having animalistic sex everyday be so bad?

He regained focus and realized she'd said "cubs". "What do you mean by cubs?"

Tigress

"You're a little slow, but that comes with the euphoria. The haze will clear. We are shape-shifters. Each of us has a form. I'm a tiger and you, my darling Jestin, will turn at the full moon. That's when your transformation will be complete," she said, even-toned.

His eyes widened and he remembered the glowing eyes in the woods that were waist level and suddenly human height. They were in animal form. She was the white animal staring into his window. *I'll be like them?* Seeing how buff each was he looked at his own chest and arms. No change, they were still average.

Yellow eyes chuckled. "The muscles will develop over time as you hunt and run free."

Hunt. He said hunt. Oh no, he wasn't a hunter. As if they could read his mind, the dark-skinned woman added, "Yes, you will hunt, but we only kill what we can eat. The cravings and desires will be so much you will crave it."

He was confused beyond speech.

Tigress

"Kyanne is our leader, as the strongest animal of the Blue Ridge. The treaty made with the humans we have honored even when they didn't. We won't hunt or harm humans unless..."

Jestin finished green eyes' words, "They bring you harm."

They each nodded and Kyanne spoke, "Your father tried to kill us. His desires were selfish. Our blood will only mingle with the human we are bound to."

"What about Hank?"

"He knows I exist and the stories of his

people are true. He will live in fear but won't cross me," she said with a stern voice.

His brain barely processed everything she said except the part about his father. "How do you know he was my father?"

Kyanne smiled and, like dominoes, the others smiled too, "I have known since you were a child and joined your father on trips. My soul was drawn to yours, but I had to wait until you were old enough --only you never came back until now. You are mine and we are bound."

Tigress

His brain exploded. "Mates. We're mates." His cock grew again. *Damnit!* he thought, *not now!*

"You respond to my libido," responded Kyanne. His face grew red and he attempted to hide his hard on. "We don't hide here. Sex is a beautiful thing. We don't live by human terms, even in our human form."

He dropped his hands and she brushed her ass against his hardness, leaned forward and rubbed. He pulled her closer to him and lifted her tiny body, sliding his cock inside her.

He closed his eyes and moved her up and down his shaft. She moaned in ecstasy and, making one last thrust, he exploded inside her.

When he opened his eyes, each couple was writhing in ecstasy. *This might not be so bad*, he thought, as his dick grew hard again.

Chapter 9

s the full moon grew closer, his senses heightened and his craving for meat increased. His urge to run grew strong. The other cats hunted at night, but Kyanne stayed with him and they bonded with insatiable sex.

The full moon arrived. The scent of the hunt so thick he tasted it. The other cats shifted, he'd seen it many times now, but it didn't cease to amaze him. Yellow eyes,

Byron, and his mate changed into cougars. Green eyes, Daniel, and his mate turned into pumas, and the others shifted into snow leopards. Kyanne hadn't yet shifted in front of him since they'd coupled.

She took his hand as the others circled them, sitting on their haunches. "Let it happen, don't fight it and the change will come easy."

That didn't sound promising, but she hadn't let him down yet. Together, their bodies shifted forms. The first jolt, his body tensed to

Tigress

fight the sensation, then he remembered her words and gave himself to it. In what felt like seconds, he stared at his mate in her tiger form and shifted his eyes downward to see his feet were now paws, covered in white fur. She licked his head. *You did good.* The words flowed through brainwaves. He tucked his head under her chin and nuzzled her.

Epilogue

Jestin never returned home and no longer worried about the Trevor Bollings of the world. He'd found utopia. He and Kyanne spent plenty of time at the cabin. The orgies didn't bother him, but his queen deserved to make love in a bed, on the table, the recliner, and occasionally in front of the fireplace that no longer burned

wood. They provided
their own heat.

He was sure the
police searched for him,
but he'd left no address,
after all it was his
vacation. The only people
who knew of the cabin,
his parents, were dead.

Nine months after
meeting Kyanne, she gave
birth to a female cub.
Jestin held his tiny tigress,
cuddled securely in his
thick, developed arms.
One day she'd take her
mother's place.

Tigress is one story from Winter Thrillz 1, only available in ebook. Keep reading for the first four chapters of Talons.

Tigress

Talons

Chapter 1

Dr. Meg Mercer walked out of the hospital's double glass doors into the brisk evening. The only thought on her mind getting home to spend an hour with Amy before bed. Within a few paces of her Mercedes, a large shadow darkened the air surrounding her, slicing the atmosphere above her. She lifted her head upwards and a chill crawled down her spine. Before she could react, talon-like fingers wrapped firmly onto her shoulders. The blade of each talon gripped her securely under the arms. She screamed and wriggled against their grip, causing a stinging sensation as the talons cut into her armpits.

Her screams of protest went unheard as the parking lot was barren of onlookers. The beast with the talons lifted her off the ground and was soon high in the air, the objects below her growing smaller as her feet brushed the tips of a small cluster of trees. She struggled against it, her feet flailing in the air. The more she struggled, the deeper the talons sank. Shooting pains ripped through her body. The strength of the beast's grasp far outweighed her meager efforts to dislodge herself.

Amy! Meg screamed as her body drifted higher into the air. Tears escaped her eyes, freezing to her face upon contact with the frigid air. The beast carried her higher into the clouds. Its wings creating a steady swooshing sound. The houses and buildings of the city appearing as tiny Lego homes beneath her.

The more she struggled, the more futile the battle was as the creature's talons only served to grip her tighter. Twisting her head, she could see nothing above her but clouds, and trees and mountains below. The high-altitude air wrapped around her body like a frozen blanket. Shivers danced across her skin and drove their icicle claws deep into her bones. One of the creature's talons drove forcefully into her right armpit causing a sharp pain that echoed through her body. A guttural scream escaped her mouth and she lay limp, hanging from the beast's arms.

Chapter 2

Meg stirred in her bed. Her eyelids fluttered from the noonday brightness of the sun flooding through her windows. Radiation traveled across her skin forcing the illusion that she was on fire. Leaping out of bed in one smooth movement she swept

the curtains together,
blocking out the light.
She could remember
the beast snagging her
off the ground and his
sharp talons which
dug sharply into her,
but not how she made
it to her bed. Perched
on the edge of her
bed, she cupped her
face in her hands and
convinced herself it
was all a dream.

"Miss Meg, I hear
you stirring and
brought some coffee.
Two spoons of sugar

and a dab of creamer
just the way you like,"
said Elsa, Amy's
nanny, as she opened
the door a sliver.

"Thank-you,
Elsa."

"You decent?"

"Come in,
honey." Elsa had been
with the family from
the time Amy was
born. She was far
more than a nanny,
supporting Meg as she
grieved the loss of her
husband and loving
Amy as her own when

Tigress

Meg had been too devastated to make it out of bed.

"Oh, Miss Meg, you don't look good. Your cheeks are flushed red like a tomato." Elsa placed the coffee on the nightstand beside the bed and brought her hand to Meg's forehead. Worry wrinkles creased her chocolate hairline and brow. "You're burning up, and what are all those splotches on your legs and arms? We need to cool you down!" Elsa ran out of the room, leaving Meg to stare at her body covered in splashes of red inflamed skin. A fever and illness would explain the hallucinations she dreamt the night before.

Within minutes, Elsa returned with a cold cloth that she placed on Meg's forehead. "This will cool you off while I draw your bath." Like a small black whirlwind, Elsa had the bath water running and was slipping off Meg's gown and lowering her into the tub of chilly oatmeal water. Meg knew better than to resist Elsa's efforts and complied.

Shivering beneath the cold water brought her back to her dream and the frozen air. She could almost feel the large talons beneath her armpits and the acute pain the creature's claw had caused. She brought her left hand instinctively to beneath her under arm and felt a hole the size of her pinky. She removed her hand and drew her arm up over her head. "Elsa, do you see anything?"

Elsa's eyes grew twice their average size. "What happened?" she asked, bringing her fat fingers to the hole and rubbing gently across it. "Does it hurt?"

"No, it's just a big hole. It feels like someone stuck me with a centimeter-sized needle."

Elsa reached over and grabbed a vanity mirror off the counter and positioned it where Meg could see the hole. She stared at it, her mouth gaping with fear as she realized last night had not been a dream. She had been abducted by something that stuck her and most likely drugged her. She couldn't go to the hospital with this, not after the disappearance of her husband and the mystery that surrounded the strange death of the man thought to have been guilty of murdering several people. No, she was a doctor and would take and analyze her own tox screen.

"Elsa, help me out of the tub, I have work to do!" Sensing the urgency of her tone, Elsa did as asked, against her own judgement. Meg was her friend but also her employer. Meg threw her bathrobe on and rushed through the house with lightning speed, not stopping as she yelled, "Tell Amy I had to leave town for a few days." Her

voice trailed off,
leaving Elsa seated on
the lip of the tub in a
quandary.

As Meg sped
through the house,
she could feel the
sun's heat nipping at
her skin even though
a thin layer of snow
covered the ground.
She had no time to
close the drapes to the
many floor to ceiling
windows that
enclosed her home.
She had fallen in love
with the large

amounts of sunlight that streamed in, giving the house a warm, cozy feel -- but not now. Today, she hated the light and the tendrils of heat that ebbed across her exposed skin. With a speed far beyond her ability, she was but a mere flash streaking through the home.

In the basement, she tore through boxes of lab equipment; setting aside test tubes, needles, flasks, a hot plate, and microscope. She had used the equipment to analyze the sample her colleague and college dorm mate -- now FBI lab rat -- had collected from the sociopath's blood. The sample had been small but enough to tell her the toxin he was injected with was unknown and deadly to him. When it interacted with his blood, within seconds

the agent destroyed
every blood cell in his
body. It acted as a
virus exploding each
red blood cell from
the inside out like
over inflated balloons.
Yet when she mixed
the toxin with her
own blood it mingled,
restructuring the
hemoglobin protein in
a way that allowed it
to carry more oxygen
throughout the body.

Meg found the
large bulging vein in
her arm. Without

hesitation, she
withdrew a vial of
blood.

Chapter 3

Several hours after locking herself in the basement and running every test she had the materials and ability to complete, she hadn't been able to identify the toxin in her blood. Her skin, on the other hand, had cleared up. Every splotch had disappeared and her skin became a couple shades lighter than its usual paleness.

Meg stared at the small sample of the toxin that had killed the sociopath. Only a couple drops remained, but all she needed was one. With a syringe, she gathered a miniscule amount of the unknown toxin and lifted it above a slide containing a sample of her own blood. She was hoping for the same response she got four years ago. She squeezed the drop onto the slide, then adjusted the microscope. It took a matter of a few seconds for her blood cells to explode. Her body shuddered involuntarily as she realized whatever the sociopath had been she was now the same.

Meg feared the worst, that she would become like him, savagely draining the blood of others. Her home and Amy weren't safe with her here. A collection of suitcases and a small overnight bag sat near the base of the steps. Unzipping the overnight bag, she collected a sample of her own blood and slid it into a pouch inside. When Amy was in bed, she would make her way upstairs, collect a few items, place a bundle of cash and a credit

card in the drawer for
Elsa to care for Amy
until her return. She
cringed at the thought
of never returning and
vowed to herself,
*Amy, I will be back for
you, I promise.*

At nine p.m.
when she knew Amy
was safely tucked into
bed, she wrapped a
towel across her face
in case her disease was
airborne, crept up the
stairs and gently
pushed the door
open. The scent of

meatloaf and turnip greens blasted her nostrils and reminded her that she had not eaten all day. She didn't have time now, but would be sure to have Elsa pack a small container.

Meg threw a pair of sweatpants, jeans and a couple T-shirts into her bag along with a few toiletries and a brush. Still wearing her bathrobe, she pulled it off and slipped on a comfortable pair of jeans and a baggy shirt. On tiptoe, she went to Amy's room and popped her head in. Amy was sound asleep. The cover bundled up to her chin; her curls spread out across her pillow. She looked like a tiny angel. Meg was near positive that her disease was passed through blood but wasn't willing to take any chances and give Amy a kiss. Her entire being begged her to hug the child tightly and never let go, but she shoved the urge aside, not willing to possibly infect her darling daughter and continued down the hallway to Elsa's room.

As she approached the door, she heard the TV in the background. Carefully she pushed the door aside. "Elsa, we need to talk."

Tigress

Immediately Elsa came to the door and, upon observing her appearance, asked, "Meg, the splotches are gone, but your skin -- it's so pale, albino pale. Your eyes too, they aren't sapphire blue, but more of a pale gray-blue. Please tell me what I can do." Worry laced the tone of her voice.

"I have to leave and I need you to care for Amy. I will place money and a credit card into the top desk drawer in the den. I don't know how long I will be." Concern and fear filled every word that spilled from her mouth.

"You shouldn't be going anywhere but the hospital. Look at you, your skin, your eyes. Turn around please."

Meg followed her directive and turned around then spun back quickly. Elsa took her hands and patted Meg's sides. "You have shrunk. Look how baggy your clothes are." Meg followed her to the mirror and lifted her shirt, revealing a body that Meg hadn't seen in five years. "You need medical care. Please, as your friend, let me drive you. We don't have to tell Amy. She is too young to understand, but you need help and medicine. Whatever this is, I fear it's worse than cancer." Elsa had seen Meg distraught with the loss of her husband but even then she hadn't looked so sickly.

Meg understood the anxiety in Elsa's voice. She felt it too. After what she had seen with her own eyes, she couldn't take herself to the hospital. She may have some type of chemical or biological agent inside her and be the study for tests that would prove nothing, while making the entire staff and all the patients deathly ill. "I can't. I have to solve this one on my own." Her eyes pleaded for understanding.

"Meg, I love Amy and am more than happy to care for her. Tell me you are coming back?"

"I will. It's my promise to you and Amy." Tears filled her

eyes and trickled down her cheek.

Matching tears streamed down Elsa's face as she reached over to hug Meg, who jumped backwards as if tazered by a jolt of electricity. Meg placed her hand out in front of her. "No." She shook her head, no, as if to emphasize the point. The hurt look in Elsa's eyes made her heart cry. "I'm sick, very sick and I could be contagious."

Tigress

That was the reason she gave Elsa -- mostly the truth. She also had a deep desire to sink her teeth into Elsa's pulsing artery. The scent of her blood had wafted through Meg's nostrils and a primordial desire almost took control. She quickly exited the room before she did something she would most definitely regret.

While Meg stuffed a wad of cash and a

credit card along with the keys to the Mercedes in the desk drawer, Elsa packed her several days' worth of food, mostly meats and vegetables. She felt Meg needed the iron, vitamins, and minerals to keep her strength in order to fight her illness.

Meg kept her distance, grabbed her few items which she threw into the back seat of her dead husband's Jeep. She

knew an all-terrain
vehicle would be
better for her trip and
maneuvering through
the snow than the
Mercedes. She had
decided upon calling
her FBI lab rat friend
to hand over the vial
of her blood. Of
course, she would lie
and say it belonged to
a patient.

Chapter 4

Meatloaf aroma tantalized Meg's senses and awoke a craving inside her that had been dormant for four years. Her female organs felt alive and dripped with passion. With a quick jerk, she pulled over the Jeep, dust and rocks flew in all directions. She ripped the top off the container and plunged her head inside gorging on the meat which felt tender against her tongue and made her taste buds water. The delectable morsel of meatloaf was only enough to send her body into a meat frenzy. She tore into all the containers, devouring each bit of meat; licking the sides of each dish until no more meat remained. When she had polished it off, her body convulsed in waves of ecstasy, a shrill scream filled with desire forced its way through her vocal chords and echoed through the trees.

When the surge of pent up euphoria left her; she lay slumped across the front seats-- spent. A growing feeling crept inside her and she raised her head, feeling dirty. Containers, lids, and vegetables were

strewn across the
seats and carpets of
the Jeep. A small bit
of a broccoli head fell
onto her nose and
landed in her crotch.
She quickly swiped it
away and looked
upwards to glance at
the headliner. It was
caked in broccoli,
mashed potatoes, and
turnip greens.

Meg grabbed a T-
shirt out of her bag
and wiped as much of
the food away as she
could. Her husband

had always kept the Jeep impeccably clean and, in only a few minutes, she had destroyed everything he worked for, decimating his memory. Her eyes welled up with liquid sorrow and short breaths followed by sighs filled her lungs.

After a few minutes of collecting her emotions, she called her lab rat FBI friend Gery. The number rang several times and just as she was about to hang up, she heard, "Hello, Meg?"

"Gery, how are you?" She didn't want to rush into, *Can I bring you a sample.*

"It's late. You didn't call for small talk. What's the problem?" Gery had never been much for small talk and had the social graces of a computer.

"Um… I came across something odd

at the hospital. I was hoping you could analyze it for me?" Meg checked the time and cringed for calling so late. She should have waited until the morning.

"You know I can do that for you. What time would you like to meet?"

"First, you need to know something about the blood. It may be carrying a virus -- some type of biological agent."

Tigress

Upon saying the words, Meg suddenly felt a twinge of guilt. "You know, it's okay." Gery cut her off.

"Meg, that's my specialty. I know you, and you're bearing the weight of a million souls on your shoulders. I can handle this. My lab is set up for it. Where are you?" Gery knew for her friend to call this late it was important and she

could hear the
urgency in her voice.
"West Virginia. I can be
in Arlington in an hour.
Meet me at Crazy Eights
Coffee?" Gery could hear
the tension and hesitation
in her friend's voice. She
knew trouble was near.
Out of concern, she
agreed to meet her. What
she didn't tell her was that
she was bringing along
muscle; her personal
trainer and brother, Kent.

Continue
reading for a
bonus story in
full!

The Calling

Chapter 1

Stephania drove higher into the mountains, her car struggling with the steepness of the slope. The ocean below beat against the shoreline and rocky ledges. The thoughts of the crazed stalker leaving her as she stared at the heavy, pounding waves. This was her first trip to the ocean in person, but not in thought. All her life she'd dreamed of it and heard it calling inside her mind. Watching the surf, she listened to it call her name out loud with each pound: *Stephania*.

She never imagined her first trip to the beach would be due to such horrid circumstances. The man who haunted her dreams until the ocean called, wiping him away and sending him into the great abyss below the surface.

She slowed the car and peered at the mailboxes. When she found 69, she turned pulling her little VW Bug into the driveway then cut the engine off. Stepping out of her car, she stretched her arms into the air and pulled her torso backwards, getting the kinks out of her neck.

She then took several
steps to the front
door and lifted the
flower pot on the
right. A shiny silver
key was there, as
promised by the man
she'd made the deal
with on the phone.
Unlocking it, she
stepped inside and
locked it again.

Instead of
dragging her luggage
in right away, she took
a small pistol out of
her purse and perused
the small beach-side

home, clearing each room until she was convinced she was alone. After strange events started happening, she'd bought the gun and signed up at the shooting range for lessons. In a short time she'd gotten very good.

Pulling open the French doors leading to the balcony, she rested her arms on the wrought iron railing and peered at the water pounding beneath her. The force behind each wave hitting the rocky ledge that held the house caused salty sprays of water to patter against her face.

Her hair caught in the chilly winter breeze, blowing her auburn waves behind her and tangling them. She drew in a large breath of fresh, salty air. It was just like her dreams. *Stephania,*

Tigress

Stephania, the ocean
called beneath her.

She gazed around
the balcony and found
a small gate and set of
steps. They led to a
flat ridge below.
Lifting the metal lock
on the gate, she
drifted down the stairs
to the flat ledge.
Stephania. She peered
below her and noticed
the rocks almost made
a set of natural steps
leading to a small
beach area beneath
her. Each rock was

wet from the constant spray and pounding of the wild Pacific Ocean.

Pulled by the call of the ocean, she placed a foot on the first moist rock, spray hitting her face from a breaking wave. The cold water brought her out of her trance and she reconsidered her actions. Grabbing hold of the ledge, she stepped back up to the balcony. She'd explore later after she'd brought in her belongings and rested.

For dinner, she cooked a microwave meal of chicken fettuccini and put together a quick salad. There was no TV so she pulled out a book, Barbara Chioffi's *Angel Mine* and began to read. She loved a good paranormal romance.

She felt relatively safe, after all, her trip here was to escape the stalker and she'd seen no sign to tell her he'd managed to follow her. Placing her book on the couch and glancing at her gun resting beside it, she stood and padded to the window, opening it to allow the breeze inside and hear the surf below. *Stephania,* it called.

Her mind recalled how it all started. First was a bouquet of red roses on her door step without a card. She placed them on the

Tigress

table and chuckled. It
was nice to have a
secret admirer. Next
the fruit basket
arrived, then the
cookies and every
other something that
could be delivered,
but never a card, and
a creepy feeling crept
into her gut and
stayed there. She
tossed them into the
trash, but they'd show
up on her doorstep in
the morning.

Then life got
stranger, she came

home from work to
find her underwear
strewn across her
bedroom. She
changed the locks
immediately. What
drove her over the
edge was when she
discovered a diamond
ring with a typed letter
deposited on her
porch. It was encased
in a red velvet box.
The letter read: *You're
the woman of my dreams.
You're always on my
mind. Quit pushing me
aside and let me in.* Her

blood ran cold and an involuntary shudder raced across her spine. Out of fear, she had several cameras installed outside her house and an alarm system. Every window and door bore a sensor and motion detector.

None of it stopped him. She came home from work to find every camera and device in a pile on her kitchen table. Frozen with terror filling her body, she couldn't move. An arm wrapped around her chest and a cold object rested against her throat. "You are mine," he whispered into her ear, his voice coarse. She unfroze and thought quickly. Her purse hung over her arm. She edged her fingers inside until she felt the cool metal of her pistol. Her fingers searched for the handle. Finding it, she pulled it out and clicked the safety off.

"Put it down, I'll slice your neck!" he demanded.

Nervous, but ready to lose her life rather than live in constant fear, she tilted her hand and fired the gun. The knife resting against her neck vanished. She twisted around, but he was gone.

Shaking with fear, she sucked in a deep breath then ran to her

car. She took a hiatus
from work and
disappeared. The past
few weeks she'd spent
in fear, hiding
amongst the crowds,
slipping in and out
like a ghost, using
cash for everything.
While using the
crowds at a bus
station for cover,
going as far as buying
a ticket to throw him
off her scent, that's
when she saw the ad
for the beach house
hanging against a

pole. She snatched it off and called.

Pulling in a deep breath, she rid her mind of the thoughts. She was safe for now. Picking up her book, she continued to read until her eyes grew sleepy and she fell asleep, her head against the arm of the couch and the waves lulling her mind into a much needed rest.

A heavy pounding reached her subconscious mind

and her eyelids
popped open. Her
heartbeat quickened
as she leaped off the
couch and grabbed
her gun in one swift
movement.

Chapter 2

Stephania stood still and listened. The pounding was at the front door. Taking ginger footsteps to avoid alerting the person she was inside, she walked to the door and peeked out the tiny hole. A woman with a covered aluminum pan stood on the

front deck of the
house. Her gray hair
in a tight bun and
lines webbing her eyes
and cheeks as though
she'd spent too many
years in the sun.

Not feeling
threatened, she
slipped her gun into
the back of her
waistband and opened
the door. The older
woman wore an
untasteful holiday
sweater with a huge
Rudolf on the front
and a pom-pom

knitted nose. She almost giggled out loud as she bet the nose had a button somewhere that made it light up.

"Hello," she offered, holding the door open halfway.

"Good morning. I live just down the road and saw you pull in yesterday afternoon so I baked you a cheesecake to welcome you to our off-the-beaten-path neighborhood."

Stephania hadn't noticed any house close by, at least not in what she considered walking distance. *I bet you watched me with your binoculars, you nosy lady.* She smiled. "Oh, thank-you," she said, taking the cheesecake. "Yes, cheesecake is one of my favorites." It truly was a favorite of hers, especially with fresh cut strawberries piled on top, but this one she wasn't taking a chance on eating. *It could be a trick, maybe the stalker is behind it,* she thought.

"I'm Mabel and I live just up the road about a mile. Every morning I go for my walk. So how long are you staying?" she asked with a smile, the upward movement of her cheeks forcing the webs beside her eyes into deep lines.

"Oh, for the week." *Lies, it was lies.* She'd planned on

staying for a while but might have to reconsider. She had no real reason not to trust Mabel, in fact she received a good vibe from her, but the past several months of her life made her wary of trusting anyone.

"Well, I need to be getting back. Clyde, my husband, he's waiting for me. I just wanted to introduce myself. We've been here for many years, so if you need anything we're just up the road." She pointed but Stephania didn't see it and wasn't stepping outside to check it out.

"Thank-you again and I'll keep you in mind." She closed the door, immediately locking it, and took a deep breath. She knew she was being paranoid, but had good reason and didn't trust the woman for no other reason than she didn't. There was nothing about her, other than her tacky sweater that pointed at her being untrustworthy, yet she was. "It's my imagination," she mumbled under her breath, dumping the cheesecake into the trash on her way into the kitchen to make a quick breakfast.

Stephania, the ocean called, long and

languid as if tempting her to trek down the rocks and explore as she opened the back door to sit on the balcony and eat.

Taking a bite of her bagel, she set it down and listened to the surf beat against the rocks. It played a melody of sorts. She cocked her head and listened to make out the melody. It lulled her, all her fear washed away with the outgoing tide.

Finishing her breakfast she closed the window, and locked the balcony door.

Strolling towards the gate, she unlocked it, placing one foot onto the steps below, careful her flip-flop was planted firmly on the wet rock, then the next.

She followed each rock-step the same way until she reached the beach, then kicked off her flip-flops and

walked forwards into
the surf. The cold
water chilled her to
the bone but didn't
stop her as she walked
further into the water
and crashed her hands
against it causing the
salty water to splash
in all directions.
Stephania.

The calling louder
and stronger than in
the past. It sounded
beside her and echoed
all around her.
Twisting in the water,
she peered in every

direction. Her wet curls plastered against her face and blocking her eyes. Her brown eyes looked from beneath the hair covering them. An area of the rock level with the ground was dark; black dark. Catching her interest, she moved towards it. As she drew closer, she saw it wasn't a dark patch of rocks but a cave.

She ran, chunks of broken shells

poking her bare feet. *Stephania.* She halted when she reached it. Horrible nightmares filling her head. It could be him. The man who stalked her. The man who broke into her apartment and put a knife to her neck. Taking a deep breath, energizing her soul, she took another step, then another, toward the opening of the small cave.

To fit inside it, she'd have to crawl.

Getting onto her hands and knees, she bent eye-level with the dark hole. *Stephania. Something* inside it called with a deep voice and two glowing amber eyes stared at her through the blackness.

She scooted back and onto all fours than ran towards the rock-steps, stumbling upward as she went. Her bare feet slipped against the wetness beneath them and she

tumbled backwards
hitting her head
against the sand. Stars
filled her mind as she
blanked out and into
unconsciousness.

Chapter 3

Hours later, she lifted her lids and peered into the fuzz surrounding her. After several minutes, her eyes adjusted to the morning light streaming through the room leaving a subtle haze. The sound of the surf was strong and forceful through the open window. A cool breeze blew out

the cream curtains
then lowered them as
it receded.

She remembered
falling, but not how
she got into her bed.
Sitting up in bed, she
padded to the
window. Her mind a
cluster of questions
with no one to ask.
Stephania…

Barely a whisper,
but she heard it clearly
as if it was whispered
directly into her ear.
Stepping away from
the window, she

closed it and walked into the bathroom. She stared at herself in the mirror. Her auburn hair tangled and messy, a small bruise on her cheek.

A sound of footsteps against the tile floors neared her room. Her eyes widened and her heart pounded against her ribcage. Her eyes shifted like crazy balls, searching for a place to hide. The footsteps just outside her door.

Tigress

She moved backwards
into the bathroom,
seeing no other
option, and looked
quickly for anything
that could be used as
a weapon.

The door creaked
open. "Stephania,"
called a man. His
deep, raspy voice
shook her to the core.
He'd found her! She
grabbed the porcelain
soap dispenser off the
counter beside the
sink and clutched it in
her hands, then

moved behind the door.

"You can come out. Lucky I followed you as you'd hit your head on the rocks," his voice calm and casual.

She sucked in a deep breath as he walked towards the bathroom. She remembered she'd placed her gun beneath her mattress for easy reaching should he come for her. It was fully loaded, but he was in her way. She couldn't get to it, not yet.

He stepped into the open bathroom doorway and flipped on the light. She held her breath and fought to control her wild heartbeat. *Walk into the bathroom,* she thought. With another couple steps he was visible to her and she'd be visible to him if he turned around. She clutched the soap holder as tight as her

sweaty palms allowed
and prayed it wouldn't
slip before meeting
the back of his skull.
In one swift
movement she
crashed it against his
bald head, sending
him flying forward
towards the toilet.
The bulk of his not
quite six foot tall thin
body hit the rim of it
and he fell against it.
Stephania didn't look
back, but took the
opportunity to run,

closing the door
behind her.

Thinking quickly,
she eyed a tall dresser
beside the wall to the
bathroom. She
pushed against it.
Since it was empty it
fell easily, blocking
the doorway. She
scurried towards her
bed and reached
beneath the mattress.
The gun was gone.
Her heart quickened
and panic set in as she
pushed the mattress
upward. Nowhere.

He'd found it.
Stephania.

A scraping caught her attention and she looked towards the bathroom. Half his body leaned outside the door, climbing across the dresser. In ragged breaths he said, "Why did you run? I had to chase you across the state, almost losing you at the bus station. What caught my attention was the maneuver you made, taking that lady's hat and slipping it on your head."

Her breath caught and for a second she froze. He finished climbing the dresser and stood on unsteady legs. "You're mine, promised to me."

She spotted a flower vase filled with daisies on the small beside the bed. Willing her legs to move, she edged backwards towards it. Slowly, he sauntered

towards her, his hand
holding his head
where a small stream
of blood from where
he hit the toilet
drizzled down his
face.

The voice called
again, faint but she
heard it. *Stephania,
come to the shore you'll be
safe here.* If she ran and
lunged at him she'd
take a chance on him
catching her in his
grasp. If she played it
cool she might get
him close enough to

knock him out. The vase itself was heavy. "Did you hang the rental sign for this house?"

"No, darling, I didn't. I saw you rip the paper off the board. You took the number but left the address and picture hanging."

She held in a gasp and let out a slow breath to calm herself.

"How am I promised to you? By who?" she said,

making her voice as light as possible. He moved closer and she clutched the vase tighter.

"Many years ago, before your birth, you were given to me in a pact. The first girl born to Malinda would be mine."

"What… what do you mean?" she stammered.

"I'm Ogden of the Earth Fae. Your grandfather and my father made the pact to keep peace between our people," he said with a crooked smile.

He's crazier than I thought. Standing in front of her now, he reached his hand to her face. She nudged it. "Then I am yours," she complied as she leaned in to kiss him. His eyes closed, she lifted the vase and smashed him hard against the head. The force knocked him to the bed and she ran.

Stephania…
Stephania… The voice
called in a sorrowful
tone. *I'm coming,* she
thought, hoping her
brain waves spanned
the air and reached
out to whoever or
whatever was calling
her. She didn't have
time to consider her
options and took a
chance on trusting the
mysterious voice that
called out to her.
Jaunting into the
living room, she flung
the French doors

open and pounded
across the balcony.

Heavy breathing
and weighty footsteps
pounded behind her.
She didn't turn back,
instead slammed the
gate as she dropped
onto the flat rock.

"You bitch!" he
screamed as his
fingers caught
between the gate and
the fence. Leaping
from one rock-step to
the next she didn't
worry about their
slipperiness, only

getting away from
him.

Jumping off the
last rock, both her
feet planted into the
sand, puffs of it flying
into the air. She
sprinted towards the
cave, her mind blind
to everything but
reaching it. A few feet
in front of her she
spied its opening.
Gritty sand flew in all
directions from the
bottoms of her feet.
Dropping onto all
fours she scooted into

the cave for safety, hoping what awaited her was safety instead of something even more fearful.

She spotted the familiar amber eyes glowing in the darkness as a large hand caught her ankle and pulled. Grabbing at the sand and shells, she tried to stop the movement as if she could hold onto them but they slipped from her hands. He dragged her body further and further out of the cave. She caught the edge and held on. The amber eyes moved towards her in the darkness. She gulped as something brushed against her hand.

Chapter 4

She felt a smooth skin texture on the backs of her hands, then a warmth filled her and she looked square into the creature's amber eyes. "Help me," she whispered.

"Don't fear," said a kind voice, pulling her inside the cave and maneuvering in front of her. A fiery desire blasted through her body. It was unlike anything she'd ever felt. The creature was so large she was squished against the inside rocks. His body smooth like snakeskin. Her eyes adjusted little by little and she saw his form. Large wings spread across his back. Mesmerized by the creature, she almost didn't hear the commotion.

Tigress

A large blast
detonated, filling the
air in the cave, then a
primordial scream
echoed against her
eardrums. Her eyes
wide, the creature
suddenly shrank in
size, his body taking
on a different form.
Light entered the cave
from the outside. She
glanced out long
enough to see the
man she feared frozen
like a statue then his
body crumpled as a
shot rang through the

air. Her eyes darted towards the direction of the shot. An older man stood on the cliff, a shotgun in his hands. *Clyde,* she assumed.

Her body eased as the man who'd made her life a living hell was blown to a million frozen pieces. The creature helped her. He and the man on the cliff saved her life. She swallowed hard, then turned toward the beast who was now a man. All thoughts left her mind except the beautiful naked man who sat in front of her. "What are you?" she asked, touching his cheek.

"Wouldn't it be more appropriate to ask my name first?" he said, arching his right eyebrow. The light behind him illuminating his fine features and full lips.

Attempting to focus her eyes on his face instead of his

delectable body parts that were oh so yummy, she stammered, "Oh… I… Um…."

He chuckled. "I'm a dragon. Many years ago I was cursed, imprisoned in this cave in my dragon form until the virgin mermaid found me."

She wrinkled her nose. "Virgin mermaid?" she asked, filled with curiosity. Maybe the stalker wasn't as crazy as she thought and there was something to his story.

"Yes, one that hasn't yet changed and doesn't know what she is. You see, you won't change until you make love to your betrothed."

Her mouth dropped open. "You're full of shit." As the words fell from her lips she remembered only moments ago he wasn't human but a dragon. She'd seen it with her own eyes. Looking at him now, he had long, black hair that fell over his shoulders and a strong jaw. His eyebrows full but not bushy and not a unibrow. An unhairy chest, full and developed. Her eyes glanced quickly between his kneeling legs and… *Oh my,* she thought at the size of his manhood.

Tigress

"Am I?" he taunted.

Their eyes met in a long gaze and they moved closer to each other. The warm feeling inside her rising towards her mouth as she desired nothing more than his lips pressed against hers. His arms locked around her.

He folded a human arm around her, his hand resting on the small of her back. His other arm followed suit as he enclosed her and tilted his head downward. She lifted her head to meet his and wrapped her arms around his mid-section. Their lips met and a gurgle sounded from the ocean beyond followed by a ripple that forced the water far enough onshore it rushed over their knees, hit the rock, then receded back into the ocean.

Tigress

This caught their attention as they pulled their lips away from each other and watched a large wave rise from the ocean, taking the form of the older woman. The tacky sweater gone. Her gray hair loosed from its bun, falling over her shoulders and covering her breasts.

"You are free Sylrath," the old lady's voice beamed. Her head then turned

from the dragon-man
to Stephania. "It's
time for you to join."
The sky above
them grew black as
the darkest night and
Stephania's legs gave
way beneath her from
the shock. She fell but
didn't hit the sand as
Sylrath's arms
scooped her up and
carried her into the
water.

Chapter 5

Stephania's eyes fluttered open, finding herself encased in the warm embrace of Sylrath. She touched his face. "How is the water around us warm?" she asked.

He ran a finger over her lips and down her chest. "We are betrothed. You heard my calls and freed me from my prison," he whispered into her ear. "The heat emanates from us."

His fingers caressed her nipples, making her shudder in pleasure. She desired him and forgot how very strange the whole situation was. Succumbing to his passion, she curled her arms around his neck and they kissed deeply.

Tigress

Her let her down
and she stood, her
feet planted in the
chunky sand below
the water's surface.
She caressed his firm
chest. The sunlight
bounced against the
water splashing
against his well-
developed pecs. This
was the moment she'd
seen in her dreams.
The calling that
traveled through the
ocean and over the
land, finding her,
drawing her to the

ocean and her betrothed.

Sylrath's hand reached into her baggy pants and rubbed against her clit, waves of pleasure pummeled her body as she groaned. She wanted him with a yearning she'd never felt before. Grasping his large cock in her hands, she stroked, but it was already hard.

He lifted her upward and eased her

onto his throbbing manhood. She gasped in excitement, lost in the surreal moment as their bodies moved together as if made for one another. If she questioned anything of the strangeness of the day's events, it all dissipated as their bodies meshed in uncanny longing.

Her whimpers met his groans as their release brought sensations of euphoria rising through their bodies. No sooner did her orgasm climax, than her legs twisted in the water beneath her, forced together, pressed against one another and she could no longer feel the gritty sand between her toes.

Peering into the water, she saw one fin instead of two legs and fell backwards from shock. The water cocooning her sprayed at varying angles. Sylrath's words echoing through her mind: *Many years ago I was cursed, imprisoned in this cave in my dragon form until the virgin mermaid found me.* It was real, all the insanity of the moment not a wonderful dream, but real. She was a mermaid and he was her water dragon.

Stephania lifted her head off the water's surface and looked into his amber eyes. "You are my betrothed?" she whispered.

His full lips parted and he spoke. "Yes. Try it out," he said, gesturing to her fin. His body changed form before her eyes. He stood above her in his full dragon form. His indigo body shimmering from the water dropping off his chest. Large wings rose from his back. She gawked as he lifted into the sky then dived into the water, vanishing beneath its surface.

Something brushed underneath her, then grabbed her arm and pulled her below the water, dragging her further from the shore. She didn't need to see the something to know it was Sylrath. They moved deeper below the water's surface. The light above growing smaller with the depth.

Her instinct was to panic, but his proximity to her smothered her fear and suddenly she was breathing in the water. *But how?* she thought. He made an abrupt stop and turned to face her. Gills on the sides of his head opened and closed, filtering the oxygen from the water. She felt the sides of her own head; beneath her ears, small openings soft to the touch moved in and out.

Sylrath let go of her hand and moved further out, his eyes beckoning her to follow. She wiggled her fin for the first time, then propelled herself forward. The water blanketed her, encasing her in security. She pushed forward, following Sylrath. He swam beneath her, circling into the air, flying high then diving, his body straight and wings flattened, into the water. Enthralled in his freedom from the cave-prison. Stephania explored the ocean, diving below, meeting Sylrath as they swam past and around each other.

Pulling himself onshore, he changed into his human form. Stephania stopped short of the beach. Her body lay in the shallow water. She flapped her fin as she debated what would now happen to her. *What about my fin? Will my legs return?*

As if reading her mind, he told her, "It's okay."

"But, my fin?"

A smile widened on his face. "Try it."

She swam closer to the shore. He leaned over and took hold of her hands, lifting her into his arms. Her eyes fixed on her fin as it transformed before her. "Magic," she mouthed. She didn't doubt that the old man and mermaid set her up, protected her and led her to Sylrath.

"Magic," he parroted.

He dropped to his knees, then laid her in the sand. His lips found her nipples and nibbled, sending sweet sensations through her body. She moaned and twisted, running her hands over his chest and finding his hardened cock. Climbing over his body, she licked the tip, then brought him into her mouth.

"Oh," she gasped as his tongue found her clit. His soft tongue traced circles around it. She pushed him deeper into her mouth, engulfing several inches as if she couldn't get enough. His tongue rolled over her clit, going into her opening for a taste of her moist sweetness. She wrapped her lips around him and took in every inch, sucking on him as though his cock was her favorite flavor of Popsicle. Orgasms shuddered her body as he continued to tease and trace around her entrance.

Grasping her sides, he lifted her off him and sat up, positioning her onto him. He slipped inside her and they made

love as the sun set.
Their moans
resonating against the
cliffs and the
incoming tide washing
over their coupled
bodies.

www.ingramcontent.com/pod-product-compliance
Lightning Source LLC
Chambersburg PA
CBHW050526190726
48284CB00003B/960